Mouse's *Adventure*
in Alphabet Town

by Janet McDonnell
illustrated by Jenny Williams

created by Wing Park Publishers

CHILDRENS PRESS®
CHICAGO

Library of Congress Cataloging-in-Publication Data

McDonnell, Janet, 1962-
Mouse's adventure in Alphabet Town / by Janet McDonnell ; illustrated by Jenny Williams.
p. cm. — (Read around Alphabet Town)
Summary: Uses many words beginning with the letter m to tell about the friendship between Mouse and Mole.
ISBN 0-516-05413-9
[1. Mice—Fiction. 2. Moles (Animals)—Fiction. 3. Friendship—Fiction. 4. Alphabet.] I. Williams, Jenny, 1939- ill. II. Title. III. Series.
PZ7.M478436Mo 1992
[E]—dc 20 91-47717
CIP
AC

Printed in the United States of America.
1 2 3 4 5 6 7 8 9 10 11 12 R 98 97 96 95 94 93 92

Mouse's *Adventure*
in Alphabet Town

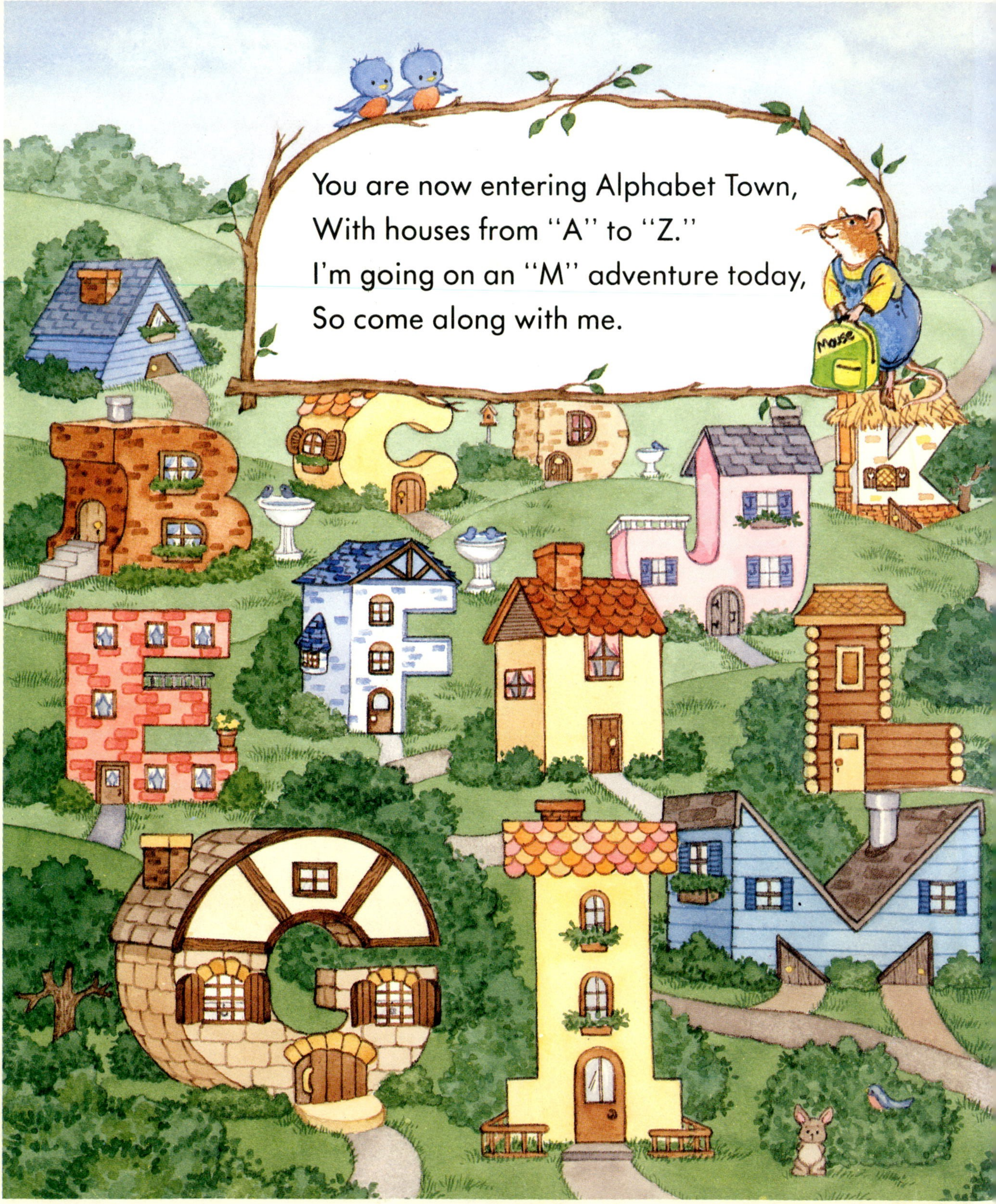

You are now entering Alphabet Town,
With houses from "A" to "Z."
I'm going on an "M" adventure today,
So come along with me.

This is the "M" house of Alphabet Town. Mouse lives here.

Mouse likes "m" things.

Most of all, Mouse likes his best friend, Mole.

Mouse and Mole share everything.
They share

milkshakes.

They share marbles.

Once they even shared the measles.

Mole, you are my best friend.
And, Mouse, you are mine.

But one day, Mole gave Mouse some sad news. "I am moving in March," he said. Mouse was most upset.

Time went quickly.
The month of March came much too fast.

Soon it was moving day.

"I will miss you," said Mole.
"I will miss you too," said Mouse.
The best friends hugged. Then in
a moment, Mole was gone.

Mouse was so sad. Day after
day, he just sat in his room.
He missed Mole so much.

"Why don't you play marbles?" said Mother Mouse.
"No," said Mouse.

"Can I make you a milkshake?"
she asked.
"No, thanks," said Mouse.

Then Mother Mouse had an idea. "Why don't we visit Mole in May?"

"Do you mean it?" asked Mouse. "Hooray!"

Every morning, Mouse
asked his mother, "Is it
May yet?"

Finally, one morning, she said, "Yes, my little mouse. Today it is May."
"Hooray!" said Mouse.

All the way to Mole's house, Mouse watched the map.

"Not too many more miles to go," he said to his mother.

At last they were there. Mouse
and Mole were oh, so happy!

They had a merry time together. First Mole showed Mouse his new magic tricks.

Then they went to a scary

They even stayed up until

midnight.

When it came time to go, Mouse and Mole hugged.

"Meanwhile, you can write letters,"
said Mother Mole.

"I will mail you a million letters," said Mouse.

"I will mail you more," said Mole.

Then Mouse and Mole said good-by.

All the way home, Mouse thought of what to write to his best friend, Mole.

MORE FUN WITH MOUSE

What's In A Name?

In my "m" adventure, you read many "m" words. My name begins with an "M." Many of my friends' names begin with "M" too. Here are a few.

Do you know other names that start with "M"?
Does your name start with "M"?

Mouse's Word Hunt

I like to hunt for "m" words. Can you help me find the words that begin with "m" on this page? How many are there? Can you read the words?

Can you find any words with "m" in the middle?
Can you find any with "m" at the end?
Can you find a word without an "m"?

Mouse's Favorite Things

"M" is my favorite letter. I love "m" things. Can you guess why? You can find some of my favorite "m" things in my house on page 7. How many "m" things can you find there? Can you think of more "m" things?

Now you make up an "m" adventure.